Rebeccah Giltrow is a writer from Lowestoft, Suffolk. She escaped for four years to Colchester, Essex, where she achieved B.A. (hons) English Language and Literature, and M.A. Literature: Creative Writing from University of Essex.

She has published her first full length novel, *Lexa Wright's Dating Sights*, as well as this collection of short stories.

For more information about Rebeccah and her writing, please visit her blog - http://rebeccahgiltrow.blogspot.co.uk

Rebeccah Giltrow

ALSO BY REBECCAH GILTROW

Lexa Wright's Dating Sights

12 Days of Krista May Rose

Rebeccah Giltrow

For Mum and Dad (and Lily)

CONTENTS

CHAPTER 1 - RINGS

It's Christmas. It's 1981. I am not yet born and yet I am very much alive. I let my mother know this on a regular basis in a variety of ways. Right now I am wriggling and twisting and making myself comfortable on her bladder. She, not happy by my movement, is clenching her muscles and running up the stairs, letting out a frustrated whine as her fingers forget how to unbutton buttons.

When she returns she sits in the armchair watching my father prepare Christmas dinner. The smell of the meat roasting makes her feel a bit nauseous so she sits at a safe distance from the kitchen; close enough to keep an eye on my father just in case he causes irreversible damage on a similar scale to his exploits eight months ago, but far enough away to avoid vomiting all over the floor.

Sally, our border collie cross Labrador cross retriever cross I don't know what else, sits at her feet, taking care of us. The low growl from her stomach reverberates through my mother's feet, up her legs and into her lower torso. I can hear everything. Her tail flaps slowly, not really in any sort of rhythm. She just wants to let us know she's there.

"She's changed," my mother remarks, "all because of you." She strokes my head and smiles. "She never used to be this calm," she continues, "especially if there was a chance of food falling onto the floor."

My father accidentally knocks some potato peelings off the worktop and as they float down Sally lifts her head but doesn't move from my mother's feet. "I remember," my father laughs, "when she would have pre-empted the falling food and would have been sitting at my feet with her mouth open to catch it."

My father walks over to us and kisses my mother on the head. Sally gives a bark of permission. He asks my mother if she wants a drink and I'm thirsty so I know she must want one too. He brings her lemonade in a china teacup. When she's not drinking from it, she stores the cup in a cupboard on its own, away from all other drinking vessels, to avoid cross contamination from the glass and the plastic and the earthenware. She takes a sip, sending the cool liquid straight into me. It bubbles and she burps. I am used to this. She gets indigestion and trapped wind all the time. It makes her body jiggle.

She watches my father as he uses every pot and pan and utensil to prepare the dinner. He knows it's pretty pointless as it will only be him and Sally enjoying the meal, but it's Christmas and it's tradition and it must be done.

Christmas songs are playing in the background. My mother sings along even though she doesn't always know the words. She's dreaming of a white Christmas, just like the ones she used to know. She leans forward to look out of the window, momentarily squashing me. It's ok, I'm used to it, but it's a small price to pay in exchange for this snuggly, warm womb. I never want to leave.

"It doesn't look like it's going to snow this year," she tells my father. The sky is grey and the rain splatters heavily on the ground. My father shakes his head. "No," he says, "it doesn't."

My mother closes her eyes and lays her head back. She thinks of her childhood, one specific Christmas when it did snow. It was snowing as she woke up. The world was different, even if just for a moment. She thinks about opening her presents. Her brothers are being boisterous, knocking everyone and everything out of the way, but she sits on her own with two parcels at her feet. Tiny flakes of snow are still falling. She watches them, hoping that it will last forever. "What did Father Christmas bring you?" asks her mother. My mother rips open the coloured paper to reveal a pair of slippers and an umbrella. She can't breathe, she can't speak. If she could bottle this very moment, she would, so that she could keep it forever and ever and never leave this glimpse of pure happiness. Her feet can't find the inside of her new slippers fast enough. The material is warm and soft. So warm and soft. She skips to the back door and flings it open with enough force to throw it off its hinges. She steps outside into the cold midmorning and shoots a puff of air through her lips. "I'm smoking," she says to herself. She pushes open her umbrella and clicks it into place. She dances and twirls and spins in the snow. She's a dancer, she's a fairy, she's alive.

My father asks my mother how she's feeling. She tells him that she's feeling ok, just a bit tired and uncomfortable. She fidgets and winces. She's not sleeping well at the moment. She can't sleep when she's too hot and even though it's winter, she's too hot. And when she can't sleep, I can't sleep. My father smiles at her and she smiles back but inside her head she curses him for getting her into this situation.

They think I'm a boy. They haven't decided on a name for me yet but my initials will be A C W after my father's father. Little do they know that they will have to come up with a girl's name in a month's time.

I'm hungry. My mother knows this. Dinner will be a while. My father is still preparing the vegetables. He's very methodical. He's peeling the onions for my mother's dinner. She can't stomach much at the moment but she manages to hold down liver and onions, so that's what she will be having. I don't really like it but I can't complain. While she waits for the dinner to cook, she eats a chocolate bar and wanders around the house in the hope that the pain in her back will ease. It doesn't.

My father finishes the preparation and leaves everything to cook. He makes a cup of coffee and takes it into the living room. He finds my mother lying on her side on the settee with Sally lying on the floor next to the settee. My father approaches and Sally releases a protective growl. My mother sits up and enjoys the smell of coffee that my father brings in with him. He walks over to the tree and pulls out a small package from beneath the branches and passes it to my mother. She doesn't want to take it. She just wants to sleep and to feel comfortable, but she can see he really wants her to have it. She reaches her hand forward and takes the package. All she wants for Christmas is to not be pregnant anymore but she knows that won't be underneath the wrapping paper. She struggles to pull the paper away from the gift. My father uses more tape than necessary when wrapping. A pair of earrings is hiding inside a little blue box. Two golden loops, unfussy, demure, subtle. She can only wear gold. All other metals turn her ears green. She thanks him and she really is grateful but she doesn't have the energy to be more enthusiastic. She apologises for not getting him a gift. He tells her that he wasn't expecting anything. She had wanted to knit him an argyle jumper but she found it difficult to sit still for too long. She'll do it after I'm born. "Try to have a sleep," he tells her, "before dinner." She tries to sleep but comfort eludes her.

My father dishes up their dinner and wakes my mother. They sit at the table and pull their crackers. My father calls them bon-bons. They read their jokes and laugh. My mother doesn't laugh too much just in case she needs to run upstairs again. They unfold their tissue-paper hats and perch them on their heads. My mother will wear hers while eating dinner. My father will wear his all day. My father's plate is overflowing and my mother's is quite bare, and yet she can't eat it all. I don't mind. She pushes the onions around in the gravy while my father slurps his turkey up like it's his last meal. She wants it to be over.

She drags herself into the living room and turns on the television. It slowly flickers to life. She's missed the first ten minutes of Top of The Pops. She plonks herself down in the armchair. David 'Kid' Jensen is wearing a red jacket with the sleeves rolled up. That's not very wintery. My mother closes her eyes. She sways her head and lifts her arms with a "this means nothing to me, oooooh Vienna". My father laughs from the other room. He comes in the living room to discover that there's a guy works down the chip shop swears he's Elvis. He shakes his hips to the rock and roll rhythm. He leans over to take my mother's hand to dance but she's sleeping. She's snoring so loudly that I can barely hear what Adam Ant is saying.

When she wakes up it's dark. Sally has fallen asleep on her feet. My mother has got pins and needles in her leg. It tickles me but it hurts her. She pulls herself to stand and, holding on to the back of the arm chair, she kicks her leg out to the side and flicks her foot backwards and forwards. Sally takes her place by the front door. She barks to be taken out for a walk. My mother doesn't want to go. She just wants to not be pregnant anymore. Little does she know that she'll be pregnant for longer than she expected. Little does she know that I'll be late.

My father walks in wearing wellies, a heavy, black coat, and a blue hat that my mother knitted for him years ago. He clips Sally's lead to her collar. She doesn't want to leave my mother. My mother stands up and walks her husband and their dog to the door. She watches them walk through the gate and into the bleak, winter night. We lean against the doorframe, letting the air cool us down. My mother shuts the door and walks back into the living room. She turns on the Christmas tree lights and sits in the darkness, gazing at the multi-coloured candles. She forgets about me for a second but I don't mind.

CHAPTER 2 - PIPERS

It's Christmas. It's one more sleep until Father Christmas comes. I can't wait. Mum is cleaning the house. She's singing along to her Christmas tape. Wizzard wish it could be Christmas every day. So do I. It's the best time of year. The lights and songs and food and presents and snow. It's just so amazing. Not that it's snowing today. It's really cold outside. People are walking past wearing big woolly hats and scarves and gloves. They look frozen. I'm not cold. My toes are snuggly warm inside my slippers.

Mum calls me into the kitchen. She's standing by the oven stirring a saucepan. It smells yum. She picks up a bowl from the draining board and dollops two giant spoonfuls of porridge in the bowl. Some dribbles down the side. She sprinkles some sugar on the top and then she passes it to me. It's really warm. I stir the sugar into the gloopy porridge. It looks like mud. I go into the living room and turn on the television. I eat my breakfast and watch A Charlie Brown Christmas. It's snowing there in America.

It's not snowing here. I wish it would. I wish it looked like a Christmas card all glittery and sparkly and white.

I finish my porridge and take my bowl back to Mum. She's still in the kitchen. She's mixing the stuffing in a jug and squishing it into the turkey's bottom. I get my stool and put it in front of the sink. I climb up to wash out my bowl but there's a disgusting bag of blood and guts in there. I drop my bowl in the sink and run out of the room. Mum laughs. It's just the gilberts. I don't want to see the gilberts again. I go and get dressed. I eat my advent calendar chocolate. It's a robin. It's yummy. It's in my tummy. It tastes like Christmas. Only one more left and that's for tomorrow.

Mum has put the turkey in the oven. The smell makes me hungry. It smells like Christmas. I help Mum with the tidying. I take all of my books upstairs and put them in my room. I sit on my bed and read. Mum comes in with some of my dolls. She puts them in their bed. She sits down next to me. Together we read today's story from The Bedtime Book of three hundred and sixty-five Stories. It's not bedtime but I want to read it now. We can read it again later when it is bedtime. It's called The Waiting Reindeer and is about a little reindeer who wants to be one of Father Christmas' reindeer but he's too small. He waits and waits for Father Christmas to call him up to help pull the sleigh but he never calls. And then one night when the little reindeer is in bed, Father Christmas calls and asks him to have a ride in his sleigh to learn how to do the job.

"Now we can't sit around all day reading. We've got so much to do to get ready for tomorrow," Mum says, patting me on the knee.

Sally sniffs around the presents under the tree. The

paper rustles. "Get off. Don't break anything. In your bed," Mum says, with one hand on her hip and the other hand pointing to the corner of the room. Sally gets in her bed. Mum makes us some cheese and pickle sandwiches, and we both have a packet of cheese and onion crisps each. We sit at the table and talk about tomorrow. She's excited but not as excited as me. My sandwich jumps around inside my tummy. We wash up the plates. There are no gilberts in the sink this time.

One of the decorations on the living room ceiling falls down. It swishes to the floor and hits me on the head on the way down. Mum says I have to be careful of the drawing pins. I pull my feet up on to the settee. Sally stays near me. Mum finds a drawing pin with her foot. Ouchies. One drawing pin is still in the ceiling and the other is still in the decoration. She gets the step ladder and balances on the top step. She pushes the pins in really hard this time so that it doesn't fall down again.

Mum gets a table cloth out of the drawer and we pull it open with a swoosh. I put it on like a cape like Batman. Kapow. Blam. Zonk. Sally gets herself tangled in my cape. Mum shakes us both out of it. We spread it over the small table. We put all the Christmas treats on there; two boxes of biscuits, the mince pies we made the other day, chocolate flakes, walnut whips, liquorice allsorts, more cheese and onion crisps, a big bottle of Diet Coke, and a tin of Roses. Mum doesn't like the coffee flavour ones so me and Dad will have to eat them. We won't start eating the treats until Dad finishes work so we can all enjoy Christmas together.

It's getting dark outside. Mum switches on the Christmas tree lights. They're so bright. They look like coloured candles. She closes the curtains and the living room is all dark but the Christmas tree is glowing. This looks like the front of a Christmas card. I don't want to stop looking at it. I climb on the settee and hang over the arm to see all the lights and all the decorations. Everything glitters and shines and sparkles and it smells like Christmas.

The door opens. It's Dad. He's finished work. Sally gets all excited and jumps all over him. He's pleased to be home now. We get all dressed up in our coats to take Sally for a walk. Dad wraps my scarf around my neck and zips my coat right up to my chin. He does the same to himself. Mum tucks my jeans into my socks and squishes my welly boots over the top. They're yellow. They glow in the dark. Dad's wellies are black. Sally sits by the door. Dad clips her lead on to her collar and I hold her tightly. Dad picks up an apple and puts it in his pocket. I don't want one.

I remind Dad about the game. "How many Christmas lights do you think we'll see tonight, Daddy?" I ask him. He thinks we'll see twenty-two. I think we'll see twenty-nine. He opens the door. It's so cold. I pull my hat down so that the cold can't get in. Sally sits at the kerb. A car goes past. Its lights are really bright. We cross the road. The first set of Christmas lights we see is ours. "One." Some of the houses along our road are really dark. I wouldn't want to go in there. I'd be too scared. "Two. Three. FourFive. Six. SevenEightNine." Dad takes his apple out of his pocket. He rubs it on his scarf and crunches a big bite out of it. "Ten." I look in the sky and the stars are all twinkly. Not long until Father Christmas will be flying past. I keep still to see if I can see him but Dad says he doesn't come until everyone's asleep. I count the stars as eleven. Dad says that's not allowed. "But they're God's

Christmas lights," I tell him. "But God has them up all year round so they don't count," Dad says, smiling. It doesn't matter. There's loads more to go. "Eleven. Twelve. ThirteenFourteen." Dad finishes his apple. Sally sits and waits for the core.

The giant tree on the corner is number fifteen. "Sixteen. Seventeen. Eighteen." More dark houses. I wonder where the people are. They can't be in bed already. Father Christmas won't come until we're all asleep. "Nineteen. Twenty. Twentyone." Dad won't win.

The beach is so dark. We can't see the sea but we can hear it if we listen carefully. Whoosh. Whoosh. Dad lets Sally off the lead. She runs in front of us. I hold Dad's hand very tightly. I don't like the dark. Dad takes the torch out of his pocket and shines the light along the path. We walk quickly. I can see the Christmas tree on the oil rig building in town. It's tiny but it's number Twentytwo. Dad laughs. He says he's won but he hasn't because we've still got ages until we get home. My cheeks are so cold. Dad swings the torch to look for Sally. She's running around. I couldn't do that. It's too dark. I'd get lost.

We climb up the steps. It's a lot lighter here. There are more houses. "Twentythree." Dad still shines the torch down the path just to be on the safe side. "Twentyfour. Twentyfive." Some houses look so pretty with lots of lights in all their windows. "TwentysixTwentysevenTwentyeight." Only one more to go and I've won. The next few houses are dark. Sally sits at the end of the path. Dad puts her lead on before we get to the road. "Twentynine." "I won," I say, jumping. I did, I won. "Well done, Dad says, giving me a hug. "Thirty. Thirtyone."

Dad pushes the gate open and I run through and

open the door. The house is so warm. Mum pulls off my welly boots and my socks come off too. It's dinner time. We have eggs, chips and beans. It's yum. Dad eats a mince pie after dinner. Crumbs get caught in his beard. He sits on his chair in front of the fire and pushes tobacco into his pipe with his thumb. He puff puff puffs and smoke comes out of his mouth. I like how it smells. Mum runs me a bath and washes my hair. She wraps a towel around me so tightly that I can't move. When I'm dry she takes my pyjamas out of the tumble dryer. They're so warm and snuggly.

I'm not tired yet. I don't want to go to bed. I'm so excited. Mum says we can watch a film before we go to bed. She puts a video in the video player. We watch Santa Claus: The Movie. I love this film. I like to watch it even when it's not Christmas. My favourite bit is when Patch makes those puce lollies that make people fly. It finishes. I'm still not tired. I hang my stocking on the back of the chair that's next to the Christmas tree. Father Christmas will know that it's my stocking as it has KRISTA written on the front in big silver letters, so he'll know to put the right presents in there. Dad moves the small table out of the way of the fireplace so that Father Christmas can get in easily. I get a mince pie from the box on the table in the other room and put it on a plate. Dad makes a cup of tea and puts it in a Christmas mug. We put them on the table next to the fire place for Father Christmas to eat and drink when he gets here. I also put out a carrot for Rudolph. He gets very hungry too.

Dad piggybacks me up to bed. I climb under the covers and Mum tucks me in. Dad reads me the story about the reindeer again. I'm not tired. I don't want to go to sleep yet. If I don't go to sleep yet, Father Christmas won't come. He only comes when everyone's asleep. I'm too excited to sleep. I squeeze my eyes closed but I'm still awake. Mum kisses me goodnight. "I love you," she tells me. "I love you too," I tell her. Dad does the same. "I love you," he tells me. "I love you too," I tell him. "Now go to sleep," Mum says. I can't. I'm too excited. The door shuts. My room is dark. I can't sleep yet. I'm too excited. I can't sleep yet. I'm too

CHAPTER 3 - HENS

It's Christmas. It's the last day of school. Miss Timms seems very excited and happy. She calls the register. Everyone's here. We line up by the door and go into the hall for assembly. We sit down. Everyone is talking. Mr Murdoch jumps out from behind the piano wearing a Father Christmas hat and a long bit of gold tinsel around his neck like a scarf. Everyone stops talking and starts laughing. Mr Welsh sits down at the piano and shuffles his sheet music. Mr Murdoch presses a button on the side of the overhead projector and it flickers into life, displaying the words to Away In A Manger on the wall at the front. Mr Welsh starts playing the piano and everyone sings.

Mr Murdoch talks to us and tells us to have a good Christmas holiday. Class by class we leave the hall and go back into our classrooms. Miss Timms tells us to sit down quickly. She tells us that we're not doing proper lessons today. We're going to make decorations and practise the school play one last time before we have to show it to our parents this afternoon. Everyone cheers. Miss Morris runs in late. She says sorry. Miss Timms looks angry. She stomps over to the craft cupboard and pulls out the Christmas box. She puts glitter and glue and paper and scissors on each table and then tells us what to do. We have to fold the white paper in half diagonally and then in half again and then in half again. Miss Morris sits next to Simon and does his for him. He's a bit thick. We then have to get the scissors and cut out shapes. Simon's not allowed to use the scissors but he still manages to cut a hole in his school jumper. Miss Morris cuts out Simon's shapes. I cut out diamonds and triangles. We unfold the paper and we've all made snowflakes. Mine is so pretty. I put some glue around the edge and sprinkle silver glitter. It really looks like snow. Simon is crying. He's lost his glue spatula. Miss Morris finds it. It's stuck in the back of his hair.

Miss Timms says that we can make another snowflake or we can make some paper chains. She brings around some shiny strips of paper, silver and gold and blue and red and green. I take one of each colour and stick them together. I do about twenty. It's really long. It's longer than me. I give it to Miss Timms. She likes it. The bell rings. It's break time. I put on my coat and hat and gloves. It's so cold and windy outside. We see Miss Timms and Miss Morris through the window. They're sticking our snowflakes to the window. It looks like winter. It's not snowing outside. It's just cold.

The bell rings and we all run back inside into the warm. Miss Morris is standing on a chair pinning the paper chains around the blackboard. There are lots of different cardboard shapes on the table; bell and star and Christmas tree and snowman and stocking. Miss Timms tells us to choose one. I choose the stocking. We have to decorate them. I stick on some red shiny paper and some gold star stickers. Miss Timms says it's very nice. She gets her hole punch out of her drawer and punches a hole in the top. She gets a piece of red ribbon and ties it through the hole. I can hang that on the Christmas tree when I get home.

Everyone finishes decorating their decoration. Miss Timms tells us to stack our chairs at the back of the room. She helps us. So does Miss Morris. Miss Morris presses play on the tape player. The music plays and everyone gets in their places. We dance. Everyone gets it right first time. Miss Timms and Miss Morris clap. Miss Timms says it's now time for the dress rehearsal. We all go into the changing rooms. Miss Morris comes with us and Miss Timms goes with the boys. I put on one of Dad's old white work shirts. It looks like a dress. He's written FLOUR on the front in giant, black writing. Carley and Sammi look so funny. They're supposed to be fruits. Carley is wearing a jumper with strawberries on it and Sammi is wearing an orange dress. Their heads are piled high with plastic display fruit from Taj's dad's shop. Taj's dad is married to Carley's mum but Taj and Carley aren't brother and sister. I don't know how that works but Taj hates it. He's got four real sisters but they live with his mum. He was happy when it was just him and his dad. He'd come in to school with his collar popped, walking with a swagger. And now he's got another sister and another mum and he can't stand it. Carley, on the other hand, loves it. She's loved Taj for ages but she's not impressed with how horrible he is to her at home. He knocks into her and pushes her and pulls her hair and calls her names and hides in her room and jumps out on her to scare her. She still loves him though. She writes his name all over her work books. Miss Morris says that Carley and Sammi look like Carmen Miranda, whatever that means.

Natalie is one of the dancers in my group. She's butter. She's just wearing yellow jeans and a yellow t-shirt. Rachel's wearing yellow too but she has a cardboard sun mask on her face. She's summer. And Emma is autumn. She's wearing brown cords and her mum's leafy coat that's covered in leaves. Charlotte's got a brown feather duster in her hair. It keeps falling down over her face. She's a chicken. Everyone's ready. We walk back to the classroom.

The boys laugh at us. We laugh at them. Charlotte stands with Marc and Stephen. They cluck *PUK PUK PUK PUK PUK PA-KUURK*. They walk around in circles, flapping their elbow wings and bobbing their heads backwards and forwards. Tim and Josie are pigs in blankets. They're twins. They have to do everything together. They're each wearing one of their mum's pink keep-fit leotards and are wrapped up in their swimming towels. Taj is wearing a potato sack from his dad's shop. It looks like a dress. He keeps scratching his back up and down the wall. It's itchy. He's a potato. James is a carrot and Ben is peas. He's got green balloons stuck all over his P.E. kit. Simon bursts one with a pencil. Miss Timms tells him to go back and sit in the toy corner. He bursts another balloon when he walks past. Ben kicks him. Simon cries. Miss Timms tells Ben off. She tells him to stand outside until she calls him back in.

Me, Natalie, Carley, and Sammi go and stand with David, Lee and Alex. Lee looks like me but his shirt says SUGAR on the front so people will be able to tell us apart. David is wearing one of his dad's white t-shirts with a yellow circle on the front. He's an egg. The t-shirt is huge. David's dad is really really fat. Alex is wearing a cardboard

17

cake on his head.

Our group stands at the side while the meat and the vegetables do their dance. The seasons are getting bored. Richard gives Peter a Chinese burn. Peter cries. Miss Timms tells Richard off. She tells him to stand outside until she calls him back in. The vegetables wait for Ben's Michael Jackson dance solo before they all jump into the bowl of gravy. It's not really gravy. It's just a big box from Taj's dad's shop filled with brown tissue paper. Ben pulls faces through the window in the door. Miss Timms pulls Ben in with one arm and pushes Richard out with the other. Ben gets caught in the door and all but one of his green balloons burst. Simon runs up to him and bursts the last balloon. Miss Timms shouts at Miss Morris for not keeping her eye on Simon. Miss Morris cries and runs out of the room. Richard comes back in.

Miss Timms looks at us. She shouts that she wants us to take this seriously and if we don't, we won't get to be in the play. Everyone looks at each other. I'm a bit scared. Miss Timms plays the music. The meat and vegetables end up in the gravy like they're supposed to. Our group does our dance and we mix the cake ingredients until Alex pops out of the middle of us. His cardboard cake gets caught on one of Sammi's plastic bananas and falls off. Miss Timms just rolls her eyes. I'm glad that's over.

The bell rings. It's lunch time. We're allowed to eat our lunch in the classroom because the hall is being set up for this afternoon, but we have to all put on a painting apron so that we don't spill anything down out costumes. We're also not allowed to go out and play just in case we get messed up. Mr Murdoch comes in to tell us that we can watch cartoons in the video room when we've eaten our food. We keep our paint aprons on just in case.

The bell rings. We go back into the classroom. Miss Timms is sitting at her desk and Miss Morris is standing at the back of the room. She smiles at us. Lots of mums and dads are walking across the playground. I see my mum carrying my sister, Jennifer, in a basket with tinsel around the edge of it. Mum's got some tinsel in her hair. I wave to her out the window. She waves back. Dad is talking to Charlotte's dad. They are both wearing Father Christmas hats. They look silly. Mr. Murdoch comes back in and tells us we're on stage in five minutes. I get butterflies in my stomach. I need a wee. Miss Timms won't let anyone go to the toilet.

I'm really nervous now. I don't want to forget my dance. We all line up outside of the hall. All the mums and dads clap. The music starts playing and we skip onto the stage. I don't forget my dance. Everyone claps. I'm not nervous now.

CHAPTER 4 - PARTRIDGE & PEAR TREE

It's Christmas. It's the end of September. The barometer needle still points to 'sunny' and the mercury has settled itself in the low 20s. Slowly, the shops have started sneaking packs of Christmas cards and dusty tinsel onto their shelves. Everything is half price and people are buying it. As I walk down the aisles, past the glitter and the sparkle and the motion activated dancing snowmen, the shops' music systems intersperse classic Christmas anthems amongst the usual middle of the road pop drivel that is played on a continuous loop. Someone somewhere has been paid a fortune to scientifically produce a playlist that encourages people to buy more than they actually want. The songs can't be too aggressive or too relaxing, just in case they heighten the emotions and cause unnecessary outbursts of excitement. The aisles would be full of old people rolling around on the floor, clutching at their chests and making the experience of shopping more frustrating than it usually is. The songs have to be easy listening, nonchalant, blah. It's called muzak apparently and there's a skill to it, and it drives me crazy. I work in one of these shops.

This morning, Mum asked me to pick up a bag of pears and some Christmas wrapping paper when I leave off work. She said she wanted to get everything bought, wrapped and out of the way by November. She says this every year and every year she rushes around half past three on Christmas Eve trying to find something nice for someone she doesn't like. I don't know why she pretends it will be any different this year.

I reluctantly buy the most hideous wrapping paper I can find, there isn't really much choice, and a bag of pears, and make my way home through the crowds of posing boys, prancing around with their shirts unbuttoned, hoping to impress groups of silly school girls giggling into their make-up mirrors. My sister Jenny is one of those girls. She's sitting on a wall near her school with her skirt barely reaching her crotch. She catches my eye and glares. She flicks me the middle finger as I walk past and yells something at me in text speak. She's delightful. She really is.

Before I even put my key in the door, I can hear Mum singing Christmas carols in a painful falsetto voice. As with every song she sings along to, she mumbles a garbled noise to the parts she doesn't know the words to. She's sitting at the desk staring at the computer. She's warming her hands against a roaring open fire screen saver that Jenny downloaded for her. She has no idea how to use the computer other than to turn it on and to set the screensaver. On the mantel piece is a little wooden nativity scene that she found at a jumble sale. She gets it ready extra early every year. She cleans every figure individually with a grubby, yellow duster. Over the years the scene has fallen foul to the taste buds of our dog, Big Bird. Mum allowed Jenny to name the dog. Big Bird chewed the head off one of the wise men, and swallowed the baby Jesus in one gulp. The centrepiece of the nativity is now a conker in a manger, who is being visited by two wise men and a Lego Darth Vader.

I notice a pile of paper, a pair of scissors, jars of coloured glitter and a pot of glue sitting next to her on the desk. I ask her what it's all for. She turns around and grins. She tells me that she's getting a head start on making the decorations. She insists that the ones in the shop are so tacky and she likes the personal touch. She throws a string of paper chains towards me and the glitter pings off in every direction. Guess who'll be clearing that up later. She stands up and asks if I want a cup of tea. As she gets out of the chair, a snowfall of tiny paper pieces tumble off her lap onto the carpet. Guess who'll also be clearing that up later.

I plonk the bag of pears down on the kitchen work top. She rushes over and rips the bag open. She has a look of determination in her eyes. She shovels a pear into her mouth as though she hasn't eaten for months. I take a few steps back just in case she eats me too. When she's finished, she spits the pips out into her hand and puts them in a sandwich bag that appears to have more pear pips in it already. I ask her what she's going to do with them. She grins and rushes into the living room. She returns with her hands behind her back. She wants me to guess what she's holding. I don't want to guess. She shows me a dead stuffed bird. It's a partridge.

She tosses me the bird and I throw it onto the table. She knows I hate taxidermy. She grabs the roll of paper from my hand as she walks past and does a little skip of excitement. She waves it in the air and knocks the lampshade but she's singing too loudly to notice. I tell her to stop being such an idiot and she tells me to stop being such a Scrooge. She's too preoccupied with the reindeers in Santa hats staring back at her from the wrapping paper to remember that she offered to make me a cup of tea.

I tell her that I saw Jenny flashing her pants to the world. She closes her eyes and continues to dance around the room. She never listens. Big Bird hobbles up to me. I feel sorry for him. He can't escape Mum's Christmas obsession. He especially hates her motion super sensitive dancing characters. He stretches and a fat Santa in a metallic red jumpsuit holding a sprig of mistletoe jumps to life, singing I Saw Mommy Kissing Santa Claus. He perks up his head when the postman comes and he has to endure Rudolph The Red Nose Reindeer spewing from a scary looking reindeer with a dodgy eye and a red light for a nose that flashes erratically. He sneezes or scratches and the whole house is filled with the dulcet tones of a squeaky voiced snowman wearing a top hat bobbing up and down warbling Frosty The Snowman.

I take him for a walk. The door latch clicks behind us and all I can hear through the open window is a medley of badly recorded Christmas songs. I'm glad to be out of there. I see Dad walking along the pavement towards me. He's carrying a box under his arm. Big Bird pulls forward and sniffs Dad's crotch. Dad tickles him under the chin and he lies down in the middle of the pavement, right in the way of all pedestrian traffic. A woman sighs loudly and takes an exaggerated step over his tail. I glance at the box Dad's carrying. It has a picture of a giant Christmas tree on the side. Dad rolls his eyes.

"Your mother asked me to pick it up," he explains. "She wants me to set it up when I get home." He sighs. "We're going to have a six foot inflatable Christmas tree sitting in our front garden for the next three months," he winces.

"I doubt it," I reply. "It'll be stolen in a few days."

He nods in agreement. "That's why she had me order four more," he mumbles, "and they'll be delivered on Friday." He leans down to pat Big Bird but he's too occupied by an ant scuttling along the pavement. I wish Dad luck. He chuckles. He tells me not to be late home for dinner. Mum's cooking turkey.

I pull at Big Bird's lead and almost dislocate my shoulder. He's a big dog and he's a stubborn dog. When he's ready he gets up and pulls me towards the beach. I let him think that it's all his idea but we were going there anyway. It's empty which is the way we like it. I let him off the lead and he chases his tail for at least thirty seconds before running after a rabbit.

It's warm, not hot, just warm. There's a bit of a breeze in the air but that's welcome. There is a boat straddling the horizon. It doesn't seem to be going anywhere. Big Bird rolls around in seaweed and digs to China to find the best stones. He sneezes and awaits the awful sound of a Christmas character. It doesn't come. He goes back to playing. I start to sing Jingle Bells to myself and then scream. There's no need for that, not in September. Big Bird comes running towards me with a clump of dried seaweed in his mouth. Tangled up amongst the seaweed are a Dutch crisp packet and a used tampon. He shakes his head vigorously to kill it, thankfully flinging the tampon back into the sea. Once convinced it's dead, he drops the creature from his teeth and runs towards a black groyne sticking out of the sand at the water's edge like a rotten tooth. He sniffs it, rubs his back up against it, sniffs it again and then cocks his leg. A minute later and the groyne glistens. Big Bird turns on his heels towards home. I'm done. Let's go.

CHAPTER 5 - GEESE

It's Christmas. It's my boyfriend's birthday. "It's so unfair," he tells me all the time. Not just at Christmas, but all the time. Whenever anyone in the world has a birthday at any time of the year, he ruins their day by complaining that he doesn't get to have a birthday because of Christmas. "Out of the other 364 days in the year, my parents thought it would be a good idea to give birth to me on Christmas Day," he tells me all the time. It's the same thing, all the time. Ok, I know his parents weren't to know that he would be born on Christmas Day, but if they were going to conceive a baby on or around the 25th of March they should have known that the baby would be born on or around the 25th of December. Or am I the only one here who knows it takes nine months to grow a baby?

"At least people will always remember your birthday," I tell him. "What? Do you mean that if I was born on the 8th of August or 13th of February everyone would forget? In all honesty, people actually forget my birthday because they're too preoccupied with the Christmas festivities. People who are lucky enough to have a spring, summer or autumn birthday seem to think that I get more presents and no matter how many times I tell them that I don't, they tell me I'm lying. Of course I get more because I get Christmas *and* birthday presents all on the same day. It doesn't work like that. My parents just wrap some of my presents in Christmas paper and the rest in birthday paper. I don't even really get birthday cards; just a P.S. Happy Birthday message tucked on the bottom of family Christmas cards," he says.

"And to make matters worse," he says, dropping his head forward.

"Your parents decided to call you Chris," I say, finishing his sentence.

"I'm sorry," he says, "I do kind of go on about it, don't I?"

"Only a bit," I tell him. He pulls me towards him and kisses me on the head.

"There are many other things I hate about having a Christmas birthday," he says. I sigh. "I've never been able to have a birthday party on my actual birthday. It's bad enough having a birthday in the school holidays but at least there is a chance that at least one friend can come over. Even if your birthday is on Easter Sunday. But no-one is allowed to come to mine on Christmas Day. It's a day for family," he moans.

"Well I was allowed to come to yours today," I say.

"But when I was little," he says, dropping his head forward again.

"You're not little anymore," I tell him, "you're twenty-three years old."

"I'm twenty-four. It's my birthday today,

remember," he yells at me.

I ignore him. "You really need to get over it. It's not like you can change your birthday by deed poll or anything," I say, pulling away from him.

"You don't know what it's like," he says, turning away from me. I keep my mouth closed. I pick up a Christmas catalogue and flick through the pages of stocking filler tack. Whoopie cushions, yo-yos, bouncy balls, finger puppets, Styrofoam gliders, parachuting soldiers, wind-up racer ducks, glow in the dark bracelets. Oh to be a child again.

"It also gets frustrating having nothing to look forward to for the rest of the year," he says. I throw the catalogue towards the coffee table.

"What did you do that for?" he asks.

"I get it," I say, "I understand that you don't get to have a special day just for you, and I understand that for one day out of the whole year you don't get to be the centre of attention, and I understand that your birthday is the worst day of your life ever, but stop spoiling the day for everyone else. Yes it's your birthday, but it's also Christmas, and your mum went to a lot of trouble to make this day nice, not only for you, but for your dad and your sister and your grandmother and for me, and look how many of them want to spend the day with you." I sweep my arm around the room. "No-one. Apart from me, and I'm not sure I want to spend much more time with you," I shout. I stand up.

"You don't understand," he shouts, "You don't understand anything."

I walk towards the door. "You're right," I say, "I don't understand anything. I don't understand what it must be like to have to share your birthday, your one and only special day, with Baby Jesus. I also don't understand what it's like to be homeless or to have cancer or to be shot or to lose my eyesight or to have a miscarriage, but I can empathise with those people because they are serious problems and they're not wallowing in self-pity. So you're right. I don't understand how tough life is for you. And I don't want to understand if it means that I spend the whole day being a miserable idiot. If you ever feel like you want to stop being selfish, come and find me."

I open the door. "Me? Selfish?" he shrieks, "You're the one leaving me on my birthday. How much more selfish can you get?"

I turned and looked at him. "Don't you ever call me selfish," I hiss at him, "I spent the last of my money buying you those CDs." I point towards the Christmas tree. "I had to get them imported from America because no-one here has even heard of Mark Murphy's 'Song For The Geese' or Treepeople's 'Something Vicious For Tomorrow', and you haven't even bothered to play them. I haven't got any money until my student loan comes through in three weeks. I also chose to spend the day with you even though you know how much Christmas means to my family."

"I didn't ask you to do any of that," he shouts at me.

I slam the door behind me and stand in the hallway holding back my tears. Donna, Chris' sister, pokes her head around the kitchen door.

"You lasted a lot longer than the others," she tells me. I let out a laugh. She walks towards me and takes my hand. "Fancy a drink?" she asks.

I nod and sigh. We walk into the kitchen. Hannah, Chris' mum, stands up and gives me a hug.

"You lasted a lot longer than the others," she tells

me.

"So I hear," I say.

Roy, Chris' dad, stands up and gestures for me to sit down. Donna slides a glass towards me and passes me a nearly empty bottle of white wine.

"I'm sorry," Hannah says, cupping my hand with her hand.

"What have you got to be sorry for?" I say, sipping my drink.

"For having unprotected sex twenty-three years nine months ago," she slurs. I laugh. I love drunk Hannah.

The front door slams. "Good riddance," Donna says, raising her glass.

"Donna!" Roy exclaims.

"What?" Donna asks, not wanting an answer. I swallow down the last of my drink. "He ruins every Christmas, and he's ruined every single one of my birthdays, and it's about time someone stood up to him," Donna says, pouring herself another drink. She slides the bottle towards me. Hannah intercepts and tops up her glass before filling mine so it overflows.

"Now that he's gone, does anyone want a Christmassy Christmas?" Donna asks.

"I'm in," Roy says.

"Me too," agrees Hannah.

They all look at me. "I really should get going," I say, feeling a bit uncomfortable about still being there while their son had stormed out of the house.

"Don't even think about it," Donna says, grabbing my hand and walking me into the living room.

Hannah and Roy follow and collapse on the sofa. Donna takes a cracker off the tree and shoves it in my face. I hold the end tightly and Donna pulls herself backwards. The cracker snaps and the contents shower onto the carpet. She picks up the hat and rams it down on her head. I pick up the plastic moustache and clip it to my nose. Someone turns on the stereo and blares out a disco Christmas remix. We dance. We sing. We spill our drinks. This is what Christmas is all about.

CHAPTER 6 - DRUMMERS

It's Christmas. It's thirty-two degrees outside and twenty-nine degrees in the shade. I'm three weeks into my six month trip around the world. I'm sitting on the deck looking out over the beach with a beer in my hand and a barbecue waiting to start sizzling behind me. Everyone's out surfing but it's too hot for me. I'm far too English for my own good. They call me 'the lobster'. The sunburn has become my natural colour now. I glow in the dark. Father Christmas could have used me to guide his sleigh last night. It doesn't even hurt anymore. That's a lie. It hurts like hell. People slap the backs of my legs whenever they get the chance. They laugh. I laugh. I cry on the inside. The beach umbrella that's towering over my head is only just enough protection to keep me cool. I'm still sweltering.

Ed is in a grump because no-one bought him any vegetarian meat for the barbecue. I don't know why he couldn't just buy it himself. He's decided to sit in the bathroom all day writing haikus rather than spending time with his girlfriend and their friends. To be honest, it's quite refreshing to have a bit of peace and quiet. I love him but he can go on. It's too hot, it's too meaty. Those are his favourites. I don't understand his meat free diet. If you don't want to eat actual meat, why on earth would you want to eat pretend meat that tastes like meat? It doesn't make sense. A few times I've cooked for him and served up real bacon. He hasn't known the difference.

Today is my first Christmas away from my family, in a completely different country. It's not yet Christmas day for them, not for another few hours. A green flashing telephone icon pops up on my laptop screen. It's Mum. I'm impressed on two counts. One that she's figured out that the world exists of time zones. And two that she was listening when I explained how to use the internet. It must be about one in the morning there. She's in her pyjamas and a giant dressing gown. She waves like a lunatic and sings We Wish You A Merry Christmas extremely loudly. She still thinks that because I'm on the other side of the world she needs to shout so that I can hear her. I thank her. She calls my dad over to the web cam. He grunts. He's sceptical about technology. He remembers the days when you did sums on an abacus and walked seventeen miles in the pouring rain over treacherous terrain to get to school, where he wrote with chalk on slate. He was not impressed when they invented quill and parchment. He pushes his face right up to the screen. I can see up his nose. I say hello. He puffs on his pipe and starts to give me a lecture about drugs. Does he not know me? Mum breaks the awkwardness with a sob and a sniffle into her tissue. I hear a door slam in the background. It's Jenny. She's just got home from a night out. Mum tells her to wish her sister a Merry Christmas. She reluctantly saunters over to the computer and waves.

She looks like her face got into a fight. She's going to bed.

The dogs want to say Merry Christmas. Mum holds up a very dishevelled looking David Bowie up to the screen. Jenny named this dog too. He clearly doesn't want to say Merry Christmas. He clearly wants to go back to sleep. Mum holds him up regardless and waves his paw at me. David Bowie says goodnight. Dad says goodnight. Big Bird is too big to be lifted up. Mum pokes him in the belly and he growls. He clearly doesn't want to say Merry Christmas either. Mum picks up the computer with a judder. I feel a bit seasick. She takes me on a tour of the house to see the tree and the lights and the dancing Santa and the dancing snowman and the dancing reindeer and the paper doily snowflakes on the windows and the dining table where she has set me a place. Mum likes to get everything set up the night before as there is no time in the morning. She has a very set regime that cannot be deviated from. Christmas is her time to do things her way. That's fine. That's Mum.

I love my family but I am quite pleased to be away from them today. Christmas at home can be quite painful. Mum insists on the whole big deal; a giant tree with a family digging up and decorating ceremony. She bakes and she shops and she fills the house with winter warmer scented candles and winter warblers singing every Christmas song that was ever released, ever. And we have to be happy for the entire Christmas period. No arguments, no quarrels, no sarcastic comments. No sniping, no snapping, no negativity. We have to watch our words so carefully, and if we slip up we face one of Mum's lectures about orphans and starving African children who would be grateful for Christmas. We heard that speech at least once an hour when we were little but now we've learnt to curb our tongues in front of her.

Dad just lets her get on with it. While she's focussing on Christmas, she's leaving him alone.

She reminds me that she would have paid for my plane ticket to return home over Christmas. I remind her that I graciously declined but will be home for next Christmas. Who would want to be anywhere else but here? At home I'd be dressed in my Sunday best, following a strict Christmas Day event schedule. Seven a.m. wake up. She stomps up and down the stairs a few times, coughing loudly before banging on our doors. Seven fifteen downstairs. Seven twenty breakfast. Seven thirty to eight thirty present opening. And it's not a free for all either. We all take turns in opening our presents and have to have a photo taken after each reveal holding the gift aloft, forcing out smile after smile. Eight thirty get dressed, brush teeth, brush hair. Eight forty-five look through our presents and enjoy them. Nine a.m. family start to arrive. First is Aunt Karen. She likes to get to ours early to get a few extra hours of drinking time in. Then Nana and Grandad who always set out with hours to spare, just in case the roads are busy. They never are. It's Christmas. Uncle Patrick and his hoard of children; six year old twins Kacey and Kai, four year old Philip and one year old twins Albert and Oliver. I wonder who his new girlfriend is this year. And finally Grandma turns up late because she gets lost, even though we've lived in the same house for years. She refuses to get a satnav because she thinks it's all part of a government conspiracy to find out where everyone is at all times. Dad agrees with her. I'm sure she goes to bed wearing a tin foil nightcap. And Mum insists on hanging mistletoe above the front door and not letting anyone pass through until they've given her a kiss. It's embarrassing.

I tell Mum to go to bed. It's late. She doesn't want to leave her baby on Christmas Day. I tell her I'll be fine. She tells me I have to call her tomorrow. I promise I will. Promise. Promise. She gushes. She loves me. I love her too. I blow her a kiss. She catches it. I wave goodbye. She keeps looking at me. She won't click 'close'. I do it for her. I imagine her crying and keeping Dad awake all night.

I look out across the beach. It's so vast, so spacious, so empty, so nothing like home. Rather than hiding away in my room, protecting myself from the millions of grubby fingers grabbing at my ankles, I'm hiding away on the other side of the world. And I'm not wearing a pretty dress and I'm not watching the clock. Although I am watching over my shoulder at my sulking boyfriend who has decided to venture out of the bathroom and is now sitting on the deck with his arms folded, glaring at the ocean as though it's nature's fault that he can't eat Christmas dinner this year. Well he can. He just refuses the repast that's on offer. He's also in a mood about tomorrow. He wants to go diving. We go diving every other day pretty much. He wants to see the fish. We see the fish every time we go diving. I love him, but he can be a bit of a girl sometimes. I love being with him, I really do, but we're in this beautiful part of the world with so much to explore and so many people to meet, and he wants to spend all of his time under water with the fish, or just wandering along the beach. We're staying in an apartment on the beach. Our bedroom faces the beach. We wake up and see the beach. Then we get up and eat our breakfast on our deck, which is on the beach. We lay on the beach all day, every day. I, to my detriment, want to go bungee jumping.

Ed has been used to getting his own way. That was,

until he met me. I won't stand for his humphing and grumphing. Either do it or don't do it. Just don't moan about it. It really winds him up. And he thinks that if he denies me sex, I'll give in. He still hasn't learnt that lesson. So not only is he angry at the prospect of a hummus and pita bread Christmas dinner, he's been frustrated since the plane took off. His loss. Apart from the sunburn, I'm having a pretty awesome time. I can't boo hoo over the small things when we're here, in the closest thing to paradise I've ever seen.

It looks like the surfers are coming in. There's Giles. He's probably the best guy I've ever met in my life. I don't fancy him or anything. He's just got the right attitude about everything. Nothing gets him down. He just does what he wants, when he wants and he always seems happy. Ed really can't stand him. Maybe because they are polar opposites. He could learn a lot from him. As well as being such a nice guy, he's one of those frustratingly good looking guys too. He's not my type, but I can understand why he would be someone's type. I could really hate him if I didn't like him so much. Adam's following. He's ok. He's just a bit too quiet for my liking. It's not that he's unsociable; he just doesn't really know how to interact with us. He's here with his brother, James. He's the same really. They're both quite non-descript but nice enough. Cally, Sash and Dray are such a laugh. I don't always get along with girls, but these ones are different. Maybe it's because Sash and Dray are gay and together so they act more like men than women. And Cally is just so funny. She does impressions and accents. It's hilarious. Ed doesn't find it funny though. He finds it puerile and childish. He can be such a snob sometimes.

Giles hasn't even taken his wetsuit off. He's firing up the barbecue. He's starving. He drags Ed up to help. It's too smoky. I can't listen to anymore moaning. I go into the kitchen and pull a lettuce out of the fridge. I turn around to see Sash standing behind me with her hand up in the air ready to smack it down on my back. I glare at her and grab a knife from the worktop. She laughs. I smile. I tell her to make herself useful and make some salad. She snatches the lettuce and pokes her tongue out at me. I take a couple of beers out to Giles and Ed. Ed smiles a genuine smile. This is the first one I've seen since we've been here. Maybe he's relaxing a bit. I turn around to go back inside. He smacks me on the bum. Yep, he's definitely relaxing a bit.

The apartment is buzzing with voices. Cally is a French waiter. She's taking our food orders for lunch. She has a moustache tattooed on her finger. She brings it up to her top lip and continues to talk with an Inspector Clouseau accent. She throws a tea-towel over her shoulder and walks out onto the deck carrying a tray of various meats.

The barbecue sizzles as the flesh hits the hot grill and this sets my mouth watering. Adam sets the table with mismatching cutlery and plates. I'm surprised to see Ed standing at the barbecue holding a set of tongs and a spatula. He's wearing an Australian flag apron and a cork hat. I never knew he had these things. They belong to Giles. I'm glad to see him getting into the swing of things. He prods the meat tentatively like it's going to explode. He raises his beer to me.

We eat. It's so good. In the distance a steel band plays Christmas songs. If you'd told me a year ago that I'd be sitting on a deck on the beach on Christmas day looking out over the ocean wearing flip flops sharing barbecued steaks with three Aussies, a Kiwi and two Yanks listening to a steel drum version of Jingle Bells I would have called you crazy. But here I am and here it all is.

James is drunk. It only takes one beer for him to be falling off his chair. He goes for a nap. He is only eighteen. I'm stuffed. I can't eat anything else. There's enough food left so that we don't have to cook for a week. Sash and Dray pack up some of the leftovers and walk towards the sound of the music. Ed takes my hand. I don't want to leave everyone else to clear up, but I know they won't do it anyway.

Ed's got a serious look on his face. He doesn't say anything. It doesn't worry me. He can be quiet quite a lot of the time. He sits on the sand and pulls me to sit next to him. He holds me close and strokes my hair. The steel drums mumble in the distance behind us. Ed's stomach grumbles beside me. I laugh. He doesn't. I watch him. He's staring out over the ocean. It shimmers turquoise and azure with flecks of golden sunlight rippling over the waves. Maybe I should take up writing poetry.

If I could bottle this moment, I would. I'd lower the temperature by a couple of degrees, but apart from that it's perfect. And I'd get some after-sun for my burnt legs. The sand is chaffing my calves. But apart from that it's perfect. He clenches my hand and looks me in the eye. I can't breathe. My heart is beating so fast I'm sure Ed can hear it. He parts his lips to speak. I don't want to predict what he's going to say but I can't help it. My brain works faster than reality. He speaks. His mouth moves. Words come out. Three words. It's like a film, softly lit and in slow motion. He's leaving me.

CHAPTER 7 - DANCERS

It's Christmas. It's our last few days of freedom. Well, it's not really, but that's what everyone says. Everyone being my girlfriends and my sister. Not that I'm one to be a sheep and follow the crowd, but they want a party and I could do with a good night out, so who am I to argue?

Jenny's drunk already. She's been drunk since Tuesday. She doesn't need an excuse. She's singing along to one of Mum's Christmas compilation CDs while sitting on the toilet. The bathroom door is open.

I can't find the cork screw. I shout up to Jenny to ask if she has it. She doesn't answer. She's sitting on the floor with her knickers around her ankles warbling incoherently into a shampoo bottle. I love her.

I wrap a dressing gown around her shoulders. She's shivering. Her face looks like it's been in a fight. Her wine glass tumbles out of her hand. It's a good job we've got a couple of hours before we go out. I walk her to my bed. She's asleep before she's left my arms.

I make myself some toast. I'm not hungry. I need to line my stomach. I'm still wearing my pyjamas. Part of me wants to crawl in to bed next to Jenny. I check my phone. I don't know why I do it. He's going to be out already. He became the stag a couple of hours ago. I trust him.

It's too dark outside. My fairy lit front window is the only one ablaze in the street. It's its own disco party where everyone was invited but no-one turned up. It doesn't mind. It's having fun on its own.

The doorbell rings. It's Amy. She's grinning from ear to ear. I don't like it when she does that. Ages ago I told her that I didn't want anything over the top and she said she'd respect my wishes, but right now I'm not so sure. Her arms are full of carrier bags. She runs in and dumps everything on the floor and runs upstairs to the toilet. She leaves a black suitcase sitting on the doorstep. I bring it in. Amy stumbles down the stairs, pulling up her tights and pulling down her dress. She spots the suitcase and laughs.

She fumbles through the carrier bags and pulls out a CD. It's ABBA. I groan. She turns the volume up to the highest number and shimmies into the kitchen. Jenny thuds down the stairs wearing one shoe. Amy squeals. Jenny squeals. They hug. I go to open the suitcase. Amy yanks it out of my hand. "Not just yet," she scolds, wagging a forefinger at me. I don't like surprises.

I hear the cackling before I hear the doorbell. It's Lise and Joanne. They are howling. Lise is wearing a headband with a dangling penis wrapped in mistletoe protruding from the top. She demands I give her a kiss. I decline and step aside to let them in. Lise plants a sloppy smacker on my cheek. The penis gets tangled in my hair.

41

Lise and Joanne continue their cackling. They spot the suitcase and Joanne drops to the floor in a fit of uncontrollable giggles. Lise rushes up to the toilet almost crying that she's going to wet herself. This makes everyone else laugh even more. I have yet to see the joke.

I ask what's in the suitcase. Everyone passes everyone else a side glance but no-one says anything. Jenny smacks me on the backside and pushes me up the stairs to go and get ready. There's no point in struggling. She won't back down. She doesn't trust me to dress myself. She pulls most of my clothes out of my wardrobe, sneers at them and throws them on the floor. She's still drunk but she behaves this way when she's sober. "No, no, no, not this, not this, definitely not this," she mumbles. I sing along to the ABBA that's blaring through the floorboards. Jenny runs out of the room. My singing isn't that bad. She runs back in clutching a sparkly tea-towel and tosses it at me. She can't expect me to wear that. She does expect me to wear that. I can barely even pull it over my thighs. That's how it's supposed to be worn. I yank on a pair of tights and a pair of leggings and attempt to put on a pair of jeans before Jenny wrestles me to the floor. I smack my elbow on my bedframe on the way down and give myself a dead arm. I want to cry but the laughs come first. She pulls off my jeans and my leggings and throws them across the room. "I'll let you keep your tights on," she says. "Thanks!" I say, winded. Jenny wraps her legs around me and gives me a kiss on the head. She loves me.

The doorbell rings. Jenny'll get it. I'm surprised I can hear it above the ABBA and the drunk women demolishing my kitchen. I'm greeted at the bottom of the stairs by Michelle wearing a fake bride's veil and 'L' plates.

I'm dreading this evening. She pulls me down by my broken arm and shoves the veil on my head. I take one step into the kitchen and turn straight around. Standing by my sink is Lise with a large glass of wine in one hand and her other arm wrapped around a naked male blow up doll. I walk out of the room. The kitchen erupts in laughter. I find a smile forming on my face. I really don't want to go out tonight. I don't want to be part of one of those loud obnoxious groups of drunk women but I fear that is what we will be.

"Come and meet Geraldo, your one time husband for this evening," screams Lise, waving his inflated hand at me, then moving it towards his mouth and making a kissing sound. I take the bottle of wine from the table and swig it back. It's going to be a long night. Saved by the bell I trip over my own feet on the way to the front door. Margot has her mobile phone glued to her ear. She doesn't even realise I've opened the door. She's talking to her husband. They can't spend more than a few minutes apart without checking in with each other. I hope Oliver and I don't end up like that. She loves him too. She loves him too. She wants him to hang up. No, he's got to hang up first. No, he's got to hang up first. I snatch the phone out of her hand and press the red button. She glares at me then gives me a hug. She's got baby sick on her shoulder. I don't know if I should say anything.

I pass Margot's phone to Joanne. She switches it off and puts it in the fridge. I drink some more. I'm starting to enjoy myself. Are we all here? I count heads. Me, Jenny, Amy, Lise, Joanne, Michelle and Margot. Seven. Everyone's here. I put my coat on and try to usher everyone out of the door. Jenny throws Amy a shifty glance. I look at Amy. Amy looks at the floor. Jenny stands in front of the door and makes an excuse that we can't go out yet as we haven't finished the bottle of wine. I hear a cork pop behind me. Michelle has opened another bottle. After the blow up doll, I really don't want to know what they've got in store for me next.

A phone rings. Margot roots around in her handbag. It's her back-up phone. It's her husband. We can hear him. He sounds panicked. She's sorry. She doesn't know where her other phone is. She promises. She looks at each of us. Joanne can't hold her composure. She laughs and points to the fridge. Margot yanks the fridge door open, grabs her phone and runs into the hall. There's no winning with some people.

I look at the clock on the mantel piece. It's seven twenty-three. I know that's wrong. The battery died ages ago but I've never got round to changing it. The green angular numbers on the video player tell me that it's eight eighteen. No-one else is paying attention. Lise tangoes Geraldo around the kitchen. Jenny fixes her make-up in the side of the kettle. Margot gushes down the phone. Michelle makes herself a sandwich. Joanne rushes out of the room. And suddenly everything goes black. Someone, I assume Amy as she's the only one left, has tied a scarf around my eyes. Now I'm scared. Everything is quiet. The music's off. I can hear my heart beating in my ears. A surge of sweat clams up my palms. Silence. A creak of a door. Muffled voices. Soft footsteps. "SURPRISE!" The light blinds me for a second as the scarf is whipped off my head. I focus on two faces that I haven't seen since I was in Australia. Sash throws her arms around me. My eyes nearly bulge out of my head. Cally grins. I can't believe it. I haven't seen them in about five years. When I've escaped

Sash's deadly clutches, I give Jenny a hug. She's amazing.

The sound of ABBA pounds against my skull. Amy grins and puts down her glass on the table. She swings into the middle of the floor and is a dancing queen, young and sweet, only thirty-one.

The front door opens and we all pile out into the night. It's so quiet. It's that awkward time between Christmas Day and New Year's Day where people are bound by promises to spend time with second families three times removed. It's cold but I'm not. The wine is working. Arms link mine. I don't know who. I'm laughing and eight others are laughing. Tinsel and a naked man flash before my eyes. A squealing voice wraps Geraldo's arms around my neck. Someone sets off party poppers. A fistful of streamers finds my face.

Four hands direct me towards the door of a dreary rundown pub. The Christmas lights in the window flicker. Most of the bulbs are dead. I pull the door open. It's empty apart from the barmaid and an old man nursing a pint of beer at the bar. The jukebox rattles out an indistinguishable Christmas song. The room smells stale and sad. I turn to leave but a wall of women force me to turn around. I'm ushered up to the bar. Someone says tequila. Nine shot glasses are lined up along the bar. The man at the end moves to a table in the corner. One two three shoot. Why do people do this? It's disgusting. The glasses are slammed down on the bar. Tequila. Drink. Slam. Tequila. Drink. My jaw hangs loose. Words stop working.

A glass is forced into my hand. I spill more down my front than I pour in my mouth. I don't even know what it tastes like. My shoe comes off. I don't know where it's gone. The floor is sticky. I want to sit down. I sit. I don't know where the chair came from. I close my eyes. It's dark when I open them. I'm blindfolded again. I'm too tired for more surprises. The blindfold isn't coming off. The room is quiet. I want Jenny. Jennifer. Jeffiner. I hear my words in my head but no-one comes. I cry. Bright lights flash at me and the blindfold is pulled from my face. I can't see anything. The music starts up. A man is standing in front of me wearing a Santa suit. My stomach drops. He gyrates and thrusts and wiggles right in front of my face. I feel sick. I need to go to the toilet. I stand up but the man moves forward so all I can do is sit back down. My body doesn't put up a fight. Flashes of light explode into my eyes from every angle. Who would want to take pictures of this horrendous man? The girls are screaming and laughing and clapping. I can't look at him. I dread to think what he's going to do. Yes, he's doing what I dreaded. He's slowly unbuttoning his jacket. He's got a hairy chest. It's making me feel nauseous. If he comes any closer I'm going to throw up on his boots. Lise and Cally dance with him. Jenny joins in. They seem to like it.

I stumble to the bar and garble "bathroom" to the barmaid. She points to a door at the back. I knock my way past tables and stools to a stinky little room with a quivering light. My stomach works its way up my body past my lungs. It takes a detour around my heart, speeds through my throat before making its yellow appearance all over the sink and down the mirror. My face looks terrible and I feel worse. I laugh and cry at the same time. My legs give way. I lean against the cubicle door. It falls off its hinges. I push it out of the way and collapse on the toilet. The seat is broken. I hurt my arse but the uncomfortable ceramic bowl numbs the pain. I cry. I sob. I wail. I sing. The words get stuck and come out jumbled.

I wake up to find that I've been using a toilet roll holder as a pillow. A hand reaches out and caresses the dent in my head. It belongs to Michelle. She looks at me sympathetically and wipes the drool from my chin with a piece of scratchy toilet paper. They thought I'd died. I thought I'd died too. She lifts me up. My leg has gone to sleep. I hobble to the sink. Michelle turns on the tap. It's so loud. She splashes water on my face. I feel like I'm downing. She pulls open the door. The bright lights of the pub sting my eyes. We're the only people in there. Jenny is still dancing with the Santa stripper. He's taken off all his clothes apart from his boots, his beard and a Santa hat cod piece. They all cheer when they see me. The Santa tries to take my hand but I wave him away and sit in the corner. Arms and arms and arms try to get me dancing but I can't do it. I want to but I can't.

Cally wraps my arm around her waist and her arm around my shoulder. She forces a glass of water into my hand. I lean against her and drink it down. It doesn't even touch the sides. I feel better. Geraldo looks quite sad, sitting on a grubby sofa in the corner of the pub. I take him by the hand and swing him around. The room fills with cheers.

"Time, ladies, please," the barmaid shouts, ringing her bell. The room fills with groans. To be honest, I don't mind. Sash slams her glass down on the bar and glares at the barmaid. Someone pulls Geraldo out of my hand and forces my arms into my coat. I fly up into the air over Sash's shoulder. I hope I'm not sick down her back.

CHAPTER 8 - LORDS

It's Christmas. It's a boy. My sister Jenny is lying on a hospital bed in a crunchy paper gown that is hitched up around her baby bump. Her belly glistens with green goo and the nurse smears it all over her skin with a contraption that looks like a large plastic penis. She giggles and swoons as she taps her fingers on my thigh to the sound of the baboon baboon baboon heartbeat.

The alien foetus pulses on the monitor next to my sister's head. I'm surprised they can even tell that it's a baby. It looks more like the first ever televised monarch's Christmas speech in 1932. A large headed creature bumbling behind a television screen. The nurse points out his head and his fingers and his legs and I nod along even though I can't see what she's describing. Jenny squeals like a police car siren and her words become jumbled and inaudible. She cries. I hold her hand and look at the pictures of babies on the wall. Jenny's ingrown human looks nothing like the pictures on the wall and I hope it never does. They're all cute and adorable and smiley. I hope her spawn ends up looking like her.

The nurse raps her fingernail on a peanut on the screen. Apparently we're looking at a penis. Never in my life have I seen a penis that small. That's a lie. Perhaps the baby will take after his father.

The nurse taps her keyboard and a screen grab of the blurry, under endowed blob screeches out of the printer on the desk. My sister takes the blue paper towels from the nurse and scrubs them over her stomach. She pulls the gown from her body without warning. I fear I may go blind. She pulls on her clothes and thanks the doctor. She skips down the corridor, like a hippopotamus doing ballet. I keep a safe distance behind her. I follow her into the hospital car park and we both walk towards the bus stop. Our bus is already there.

Jenny lowers herself awkwardly into a seat designated for the elderly, infirm, disabled and women who can't keep their legs closed at the front of the bus. She doesn't look as pregnant as she thinks she does. She looks like she's eaten a bit too much Mexican food. She's not glowing. She's bloated and sweaty. There is no-one else on the bus apart from us. I go to sit down next to her and she shakes her head, pointing to the picture of a fat stick-woman on the wall. I sit behind her. She fingers the buttons on her coat and smiles to herself. The picture will be dog-eared before she gets home.

She hurries off the bus when it gets to town. She's hungry. She wants a tuna niçoise salad. She also needs to pee. She waddles to the toilets at the other end of the supermarket. There are no tuna niçoise salads in the fridge so she will have to make do with a tuna mayonnaise sandwich, an egg mayonnaise sandwich, a jar of olives, and a packet of crisps. I wait for her by the door. Two ducks walk across the car-park's zebra crossing. Who knew that birds were such law abiders. I pass her the carrier bag. She pushes my arm away. She feels sick and can't face eating anything. I open one of the sandwiches and leave it on the ground for the ducks.

Jenny gravitates towards the department store. I reluctantly follow her. I could quite happily leave her alone but I don't want to hear what a terrible sister I am, leaving a pregnant woman alone. She has a focussed stride in her step as she makes her way to the escalator, knocking into a display of faux fur handbags. The orange lady at the make-up counter glares. Well I think she glares. I can't really make out what her eyes are doing behind her spider leg eyelashes. I saunter two steps behind Jenny to stay out of the line of fire.

She pulls me towards the baby clothes. My eyes plead for someone to save me but no-one dares get in the way of a determined pregnant lady. She pulls cutesy outfits from the rails and holds them up to her stomach. I can't have children. She's too occupied with her own pregnancy to remember that. Her fingers touch tiny red and white Santa hats and mini Christmas pudding onesies. It makes me feel hungry. I open the jar of olives.

She carries an armful of garments towards the till. She drops the star hat that tops the Christmas tree ensemble. The palms of the mittens are baubles and there's a tinsel scarf. She looks at me and then at the yellow scrap of material at her feet and then back at me. A pre-pubescent boy wearing an ill-fitting suit with a walkie-talkie strapped to his belt rushes over to her before I can reach her and picks up the stellar hat. He glances back at me and ushers her over to a plush purple pouffe next to a display of I Love My Mummy / Daddy / Nanny / Grandad / Second Cousin Twice Removed babygrows.   She's wearing a poncho and moccasins.   She stretches her legs forward and flexes her toes up and down. "Swollen ankles," she tells a disinterested elderly couple who walk past, giving her a wide berth so she doesn't kick them.   The old man nods and tosses her a half smile.   The old woman does nothing.   I love her but sometimes I wish I didn't.   I feel like walking away from the centre of the universe.   Apparently it's expanding daily.   Maybe it will explode.

She feigns tiredness and holds the clothes up to me. I pay for the overpriced things that her child will never wear. He's due in February. By the time his first Christmas comes around he'll be too big to be a new-born Christmas tree. I'll take the money out of her purse when she falls asleep later.

Jenny eats the crisps and drinks the olive juice while waiting for the bus. If that isn't disgusting enough, she shows her ultrasound picture to everyone else in the queue. A piece of crisp is caught in her hair. I don't tell her. I check my watch. The bus should be here in a few minutes. If I ignore her, she might go away. She doesn't. An old man steps aside and let's Jenny get on the bus. He steps right in front of me, stands on my foot and doesn't even apologise. I hear her voice saying, "My sister is paying for me." I count my change and can just about manage to pay for both of us. I'd like to put this down to her hormones but she's always been this generous.

Mum looks like she's just won the lottery. She claps her hands which sets off the noise activated singing Father Christmas on the coffee table. He shudders his hips from side to side and "Here Comes Santa Claus" spews from his lock-jaw mouth. She knows how much I hate that thing and no matter how many times I take the batteries out, it still manages to find its voice. Mum grabs Jenny's hands and twirls her around. I laugh imagining her throwing up mid spin. They both can't stop smiling. "This is the best Christmas present ever," Mum beams. I glance over at the dining table to the papier-mâché fruit bowl that I made fourteen Christmases ago. She tosses me a disparaging look as she leans her head towards Jenny's abdomen. She uncomfortably nuzzles her ear into her belly button. "He's kicking. It sounds like ten lords are leaping in there. He'll be a dancer for sure, tapping his toes in a Broadway musical." She looks back up at me with disappointment. I walk out of the room. She doesn't know I can't have children. It's not her fault.

Dad taps me on the left shoulder. I turn around. He isn't there. He's on my right. He tells me that my time will come soon. It won't. I tell him. He hugs me. He smells of cigars and Belgian chocolate. I shrug. I never wanted children anyway. I've got a dog. That's more than enough. Who wants a baby nowadays anyway?

She wants to call him Valentino. She hasn't even told his father. He knows she's pregnant. He just doesn't know it's a boy. Not that it should matter anyway. I ask her if she's told him. She'll do it later. She's tired. She goes upstairs for a nap. I pull her purse out of her handbag and shove a wad of twenty pound notes into my purse. Mum's on the phone telling the world and his wife about Valentino. "He's so handsome. He's going to be a heart breaker. I can just tell." I glance over her shoulder and look at the blurry ultrasound picture. I think she's holding it upside down.

The front door clicks behind my goodbye. My

pocket vibrates. It's Oliver. He doesn't want anything in particular. I tell him that I'll be home in about fifteen minutes. The bus is a minute late. It's empty. I don't like getting on empty buses. I press nine nine on my phone and hold it in the palm of my hand. No one gets on at the next stop. Or the next one. Or the next one. An old woman gets on at the next one. I clear my phone's screen. She's pushing a tartan fabric trolley. The wheels are muddy. She's wearing a badge in the shape of a Christmas tree. It has flashing lights. She wishes me a Happy Christmas. I nod and smile back, "You too." A woman follows her. She's got long hair and a limp. The old woman sits behind me. She smells of wine. It's nauseating.

The night has overtaken the day. The streetlights look like stars. More people get on the bus. A child drops a bag of sweets on the floor. Coloured balls rattle around under the seats. The child gets on his knees and starts to pick up the sweets and put them in his mouth. His mother lets him.

Oliver and Miss Marple are waiting for me at the bus stop. She tries to run on the bus when the door opens. Her tail is wagging manically and her eyes are bulging out of her face as she pulls towards me. It's nice to know that someone is pleased to see me. Oliver kisses my head. I take Miss Marple's lead. Oliver wraps his arm around my shoulder and pulls me into his chest. It's warm there. He gives me his gloves. Miss Marple zigzags across the pavement and ties up my legs with her lead. This is my family.

CHAPTER 9 - SWANS

It's Christmas. It's half past ten in the morning. We're at Oliver's parents' house this year. They're a bit posh and their house is far too clean and tidy for my liking. They have paper coasters that they put over the normal coasters so that they don't get dirty.

I'm perched on the edge of their cream and beige sofa holding on to my mug of tea with dear life so as not to spill a drop of brown liquid on their pale oatmeal carpet. Miss Marple isn't welcome here with her grubby paws and messy eating habits so she's spending Christmas with my parents. They don't mind. They miss having a dog in the house since Big Bird and David Bowie died so I know they'll make a fuss of her.

It's not that his parents are horrible. They just have routines and a system where things have their specific place and one millimetre out of place will not be tolerated. I finish my tea and put the mug down on the coastered coaster. Malcolm, Oliver's dad, tosses the mug a glance before looking at me then back at the mug. I stand up, pick up the mug and take it into the kitchen. I rinse it out in the sink with hot water and then put it in the dishwasher on the top shelf starting from the back.

I return to the sofa to find the cushion I had been using has been moved back to its place in the middle of the seat. I rest it on the arm of the sofa, lay my head down and close my eyes. I'm so tired. I really don't sleep well when I'm not in my own bed and Margie, Oliver's mum, was banging around in the kitchen at stupid o'clock this morning so I could do with a nap now. I'd like to have a proper lay down but you're not allowed to put your feet on the chairs. She's still at it. She won't let anyone help her but the noises from the kitchen suggest that she's not coping very well.

My feet are cold. I look at the ugly grandma slippers that Malcolm and Margie bought for me, sitting under the perfectly symmetrical tree. My feet are really cold but I really don't want to wear them. I'm not being ungrateful but they are so ugly. I put them on but accidentally knock the tree when I stand up. An ornament falls off. I hold my breath. It doesn't break. I pick it up and hang it back on a branch. Malcolm walks over to the tree and moves the ornament to one branch higher up. I apologise. Oliver gives me a half smile. I just hope he doesn't turn out like this in his old age.

Oliver is reading a book that his parents bought him for Christmas and Malcolm is thumbing through a magazine about whittling. I know he's not really reading it because it keeps looking at me suspiciously, making sure I don't put anything else out of place. The silence is interrupted by a smash and an "oh fiddlesticks". Oliver touches my leg and hurries into the kitchen only to be shooed back out. There's a knock at the door. I get up. Maybe a burst of fresh air will wake me up. Oliver's sister, Elizabeth, is in the porch looking flustered trying to manoeuvre a twin pushchair through the door. Her husband, Julian, can't be seen behind a giant baby cage full of oversized cuddly toys. They crash and bang their way through the house and make their way up to Elizabeth's old bedroom. I carry up the bags that they leave in the hallway. Julian puts the baby cage over by the window and Elizabeth lowers Felix and Emily onto their giant teddy bear pillows. We creep out of the room so as not to wake them.

Elizabeth stands on the landing and rests her hands on the banister. She looks at me with extremely tired eyes. Normally she looks so glamorous but today she is a dishevelled wreck. "The babies. The babies were up all night crying. They alternated so that when one had settled back down to sleep, the other started," she tells me. "You're so lucky that you don't have children. You don't know how lucky you are." Yes, I'm so lucky.

Margie is pacing the hallway sipping a glass of sherry. She has blue plasters wrapped neatly around three of her fingers. She didn't have those earlier this morning. Elizabeth wanders to the conservatory. She doesn't even say hello to her parents. She squeezes her feet into her mother's welly boots, wraps a shawl around her shoulders and mumbles something about needing to be alone. Julian goes to follow her but she shuts the door in his face. He turns around and forces a smile.

Margie calls Oliver into the kitchen. He looks worried. He's only in there for about a minute. He comes out carrying a wooden crate that looks like a pirate's treasure chest. He struggles into the dining room. Julian and Malcolm are talking business in the study. They shut the door so as not to be disturbed. I go into the dining room. Oliver is wearing white cotton gloves and is removing a white table cloth from a vacuum packed plastic bag. I walk forward to help him. He steps back. The table cloth can only be unfolded if white gloves are worn. I laugh. He's deadly serious. I take a seat at the head of the table. I'm such a rebel.

I watch Oliver's brow furrow with concentration. It takes him five minutes to straighten the table cloth. He takes a metal ruler from the crate and lays it across the centre of the table. He buffs a silver candlestick with the heel of his hand and puts it in the middle of the table. Two glass bowls come out of the crate next. He sets them down equidistant from the candlestick. This takes a couple of minutes to be exact. He fills the bowls with freshly cut holly. Each bowl contains the same number of leaves and berries. OCD much.

Placemats and cutlery take forever to lay. Water glasses. Wine glasses. Finger bowls. Fish forks. Soup spoons. Lobster crackers. Snail tongs. Oyster knives. "Don't worry. We won't be using all of these implements of torture," he smiles. That's good. I wouldn't know how to use them. Margie comes in and a spark of joy rushes across her face. She skips up to Oliver, squeezes his arm and gives him a kiss on the cheek. "It's perfect," she whispers. She takes the empty crate from him and returns holding a perfectly folded napkin swan. She puts it on Malcolm's placemat, beak facing the chair. She makes the same trip five more times. I don't dare breathe. It looks like one of those replica Victorian tables in a museum. All it needs are those scary mannequins with dusty top hats and unblinking eyes to complete the scene.

Oliver calls Elizabeth in from the garden. She's

sniffing and her cheeks are all red. I don't know if she's been crying or she's just cold. She doesn't say anything. No-one says anything. Malcolm sits down at the head of the table. He moves his placemat a couple of millimetres to the left. Everyone else sits down apart from Margie who scurries to the kitchen. Julian puts a white plastic baby monitor on the table next to his wine glass. He twiddles the volume knob. We can hear the faint breathing of the babies. It's quite relaxing. Malcolm coughs, tuts and shakes his head. Julian puts the monitor on the floor by his feet. Malcolm sighs. This Christmas feels so unChristmassy. It makes me sad.

I quietly comment to Oliver about Christmas crackers. Malcolm hears. "We don't have crackers. They're extremely tacky and unnecessary," he comments. I've never known fun to be unnecessary. I chuckle to myself thinking of my dad in his tacky and unnecessary tissue paper hat that he will wear from lunch time until bedtime. He'll read out the jokes without his glasses on so he'll read them wrong and mistime the punch line. There'll be laughter and silliness and warmth. I wish I was there. I reach across and squeeze Oliver's hand. He's sitting upright. He squeezes my hand back but he doesn't look at me. It's going to be a long lunch.

Margie brings in plates of food. She puts them down in the middle of the table. We help ourselves. I'm the only one to thank her. I feel uncomfortable for doing it. We eat. It's like a morgue in here. One of the babies starts crying. Malcolm throws his fork down onto his plate. Julian hurries upstairs. His socked feet pad the carpet along the landing. We hear him singing to the children. He's got quite a nice voice if I'm honest. I rarely hear him say anything. He laughs. The babies giggle. It's refreshing. Elizabeth leans down and switches off the monitor. We fall back into silence.

The food is delicious. I'm not a huge fan of gravy dinners, but you can't beat Christmas dinner with all the trimmings. I pass on the sprouts though. I lean back in my chair, stuffed to burst. I really want to undo the buttons on my trousers and give my stomach some breathing room, but that's not dining room etiquette. Not that I really know what dining room etiquette is, but here I always go against my natural instincts to be on the safe side.

Margie clears the plates herself, rejecting my offer of help. Julian hurries back down. His plate has been taken away. He hadn't finished his meal. Margie wheels a three-shelved hostess trolley into the room. On the top shelf are bowls and two jugs. "Cream," she says pointing to one. "Custard," she says, pointing to the other. She puts the jugs on the table, and lists the desserts on the trolley like she's a waitress in a restaurant. "You've got a choice of homemade mince pies, homemade Christmas pudding, homemade Bûche de Noël ..."

"That's a yule log," Oliver whispers to me. I nod.

"... homemade Christmas cake, homemade sherry trifle, homemade gingerbread cookies, homemade crème brûlée, homemade panna cotta, homemade panettone, and homemade vanilla cheesecake." She sighs and shifts her weight to her other foot as she leans against the trolley. She looks tired. I'm not surprised with all of those homemade treats in front of us. Malcolm wipes his mouth with his napkin and puts it on the table. "I'm not hungry," he says, standing up and leaving the room. I feel so sorry for Margie. I'm not hungry but I ask for some mince pies and custard.

Margie smiles as she passes me the bowl. I pour a golden slurry over my pies and attack them with a spoon. They're delicious. Not as nice as the mince pies I used to make with Mum, but they're nice nonetheless.

Julian picks up the baby monitor and turns it on. It's quiet. He takes a slice of cake, a bowl of trifle and three cookies. He must be hungry. Elizabeth walks out of the room without saying anything. We hear the back door click close. Oliver takes his tired mother's hand and leads her out of the room. She must be shattered. I hope he's taking her to bed so that she can sleep the day away. I push my bowl away from me. I can't eat anything else. I smile awkwardly at Julian. The silence is broken by a soft cry from the baby monitor.

"Not again," Julian sighs, sliding his chair back. "I'll go," I say. I walk up the stairs; I'm still too full to run. I pick up Emily. She stops crying. I sit on the floor and lean up against the bed. She smacks her tongue against her lips and closes her eyes. I run my hand over her soft hair and breathe her in. I don't know how lucky I am.

CHAPTER 10 - MILKING MAIDS

It's Christmas. It's the first day of the sales. Jenny is bundling her brood into the back of her people carrier. Valentino refuses to get dressed. Jenny shoves a pair of welly boots into my hand and points to her son. I force his feet into the boots and wrap a coat around his Superman pyjamas. I don't dare let go of him. I don't know where he'd end up. Jenny comes in and carries him under her arm to the car. She straps him into his seat and receives a kick to the face. She gives him a bar of chocolate to keep him quiet. Merry-Belle is sleeping next to him. Even when he sticks his half eaten chocolate bar into her ear she stays asleep. Cherry Cola is sucking her thumb and reading a book, and when I say book, I mean one of her mother's trashy celebrity magazines, and when I say read, I mean she's turning the pages and laughing, and when I say turning the pages, I mean she's chewing on the paper. It's keeping her quiet so I don't mind. I spray anti-freeze onto the windscreen and scrape the ice off. It seeps through my gloves.

Jenny wrestles with the easy to fold double

pushchair. I don't offer to help. I'm still nursing my hand since the last time it attacked me. She slams the boot closed. Merry-Belle wakes up and starts crying. Jenny shoves a bar of chocolate into her mouth. She stops crying. Jenny runs back into the house. I look at my watch. It's seven thirty-two. My eyes feel like they're bleeding. Jenny hurries out mumbling something about being behind on the schedule. She has a yellow papoose wrapped around her torso with a wriggling Origami trying to escape the suffocating fabric. She drags a suitcase sized baby bag along the path. It gets caught on a gnome display. The bag pops open and a baby bottle of milk rolls out. Valentino screams for his boo-boo boo-boo. For a six year old, his grasp of the English language is seriously below par. Jenny picks up the bottle and passes it to me. "Give Valenteeny-weeny his banana breast milk breakfast milkshake," Jenny garbles. My jaw drops. Valentino's arms nearly pop out of their sockets trying to grab for the bottle. He loves it. He won't drink ordinary cow's milk. I can't believe I hadn't noticed his eating habits sooner. Silly me for assuming my sister would do things properly. Valentino chows down on his delightful cocktail. Jenny dumps her bag on to the passenger side footwell and climbs in after it. Looks like I'm driving then. She pulls the seatbelt across her chest, pushing Origami even closer to her bulging bosom. I'm sure that's against the law. "She won't sit in the back with her brother and sisters. She can't bear to be alone," Jenny says in a sing-song voice. "She won't be alone. She'll be with her brother and sisters," I tell her. "She wants to be with her mummy," Jenny mumbles at her chest.

My view is distorted by the Christmas tree decorations hanging from the rear view mirror. I untangle the baubles and singing reindeer from my line of sight. Jenny calls me a Scrooge. It's clear which parent she's taken after. I'd rather be a Scrooge than kill us all because I can't see. I shove the decorations into the glove compartment. I get a "bah humbug" from Jenny, a "boo-boo humbug" from Valentino and a "bum bumbug" from Cherry Cola. I pull out of the drive way, seven minutes past the scheduled leaving time. Valentino has finished his drink and has decided to play football with the back of my chair. I tell him to stop. My sister tells me to stop telling him to stop. He gets bored with kicking my chair so he hits Merry-Belle with his empty bottle. Merry-Belle lets out the highest pitched scream I've heard in a long while. Jenny doesn't notice. She's fallen asleep to the sound of whale song pumping through her i-pod earphones. She's got the volume turned up so loud that I can hear it too. I reach down into her bag and pull out a handful of mini chocolate bars and throw them behind me. Silence. Beautiful.

The roads are clear. I guess all normal people are still in bed. I splash through the street lit puddles and make my way across town. The traffic starts to build up. I can see the shopping centre car park. It's about five hundred metres away. It should only take two minutes to get there. I stop behind a car that has stopped behind a car that has stopped behind a long queue of cars. I pull on the handbrake. Valentino kicks my chair again. Jenny is still asleep. I turn around and smack him on the leg. I don't agree with smacking children but I will make an exception every now and then. The car behind honks its horn. Four children and a grown woman fill the car with various degrees of noise. Valentino wants more boo-boo. Cherry Cola is squealing for no other reason than she likes the sound of her own squeal.

Merry-Belle is copying her sister. They compete to see who can be the loudest. Origami just cries. Jenny complains about the traffic and the rudeness of people coming out this early in the morning and blocking the road for everyone else. The car behind honks again. Jenny opens her window and screams expletives over her shoulder. Valentino takes it upon himself to repeat his mother's colourful language. Cherry Cola copies him. An adorable "fufis bassin" falls out of her mouth. I try not to laugh but she's too cute. I slap Jenny on the knee. She swears at me. I have to bite my tongue.

The traffic moves slowly. I click the handbrake down. I stall the car. Jenny glares at me. I'm too tired to argue. I pull away and follow the train of cars pootling along in second gear. Jenny plugs her i-pod into the stereo. We all get the pleasure of hearing whales mating. Cherry Cola sings along and Merry-Belle copies her. We stop again. I want to get out of the car and walk. Origami continues to cry. Jenny unclicks her seatbelt and pulls her baby out of the papoose. She shuffles out of her top and pulls a breast free from the confines of her maternity bra. Two men walk past and nearly break their necks looking through our car window. "Aw'wite darlin', got any of that for us." She turns the volume knob down and stares at the man without covering herself up. She plonks Origami on my lap and leans out the window. She yells at the men, aiming her breast at them. "Come on then. What are you waiting for? You want some? Come and get it then. There's loads to go round," she screams. The men laugh nervously and walk off. "Nah, you're aw'wite love." I cover my face with my hand. She snatches her baby from me and shoves her nipple in Origami's mouth. She suckles as though she's been starved. Valentino sees his sister and yells for his boo-boo from the back seat. His other sisters join in the chorus for boo-boo, their arms grabbing forwards as they strain to leave their car seats. Jenny nudges the bag with her knee. I pull out three bottles of milk and pass them back. The animals scavenge for their food. I almost lose a finger.

I edge forward. The town's decorations look sad and dishevelled in the mid-morning light. An orange traffic cone adorns the top of the Christmas tree and the street nativity scene's Mary is now a blow-up doll modestly wearing a Santa hat and nothing else. Jenny finds this hilarious. An idiot is trying to bypass the queues by overtaking everyone on the wrong side of the road. I keep unhealthily close to the car in front. The idiot flicks on his indicator and attempts to squeeze in. No-one moves to let him in. He gets angry. He zooms off down the road and almost gets ploughed into by a bus. Serves him right. The queue splits. Jenny navigates. "Go left. Go left. Left. Left. Left." I go left. "Stay left. Stay left." I can't go in any other direction. There are cars surrounding us from every angle. The gaping hole of the multi-storey car park entrance swallows the car in front of the car in front. We're separated from the car in front by the security barrier. I roll down my window, lean out and press the button. The machine spits a ticket out at me. The arm raises and lets me through. All I can see are cars. Parked cars and cars looking for somewhere to park. I can't see any empty spaces. Jenny takes it upon herself to start navigating again. "Go to the parent and child spaces. Go to the parent and child spaces. The parent and child spaces." I can only move as fast as the car in front and the car in front isn't moving. "It's straight down there. Down there. On the right. Just past the stairs.

On the right." I can see from here that there are no spaces on the right. I drive quickly up the slope. I get an earful of abuse from a woman who is still half naked in the front seat of our car.

On the eighth floor the navigator spots a space. "In there. In there. There. Next to the red car. The red one. The red car just there." I don't know if she's ever successfully parked a monster truck in a shoe box with a fog horn blaring in her ear but I'm clearly not that skilled. The eleventh floor is empty apart from a red sports car that has been selflessly parked over two spaces. I manoeuvre as best as I can into the space but it's not good enough. I don't care. I get out of the car. The vast concrete landscape makes it feel colder than it actually is. Tiny speakers by the stairwells squeeze out tinny panpipe renditions of classic Christmas songs. Jenny sings the wrong words to Silent Night. The tune playing is Away In A Manger.

I take a deep breath and open the boot. The easy to fold pushchair jumps out and unfolds without me having to touch it. Both Cherry Cola and Merry-Belle are asleep. I unclip Merry-Belle from her control harness and she lollops into my arms. She smells sweet and delicious. I don't want to put her down. I hold her close and breathe her in. She's so small. I slip her into the pushchair and wrap a blanket around her. It eats her up. Cherry Cola yawns but her eyes stay closed. She's not as small as her sister but she smells just as sweet. She snuggles up next to Merry-Belle. I leave Valentino's disembarkment for his mother. I don't dare move him. I don't fancy losing a limb, not today.

Jenny appears from the other side of the car fully dressed with Origami back in her uncomfortable baby sling. A leg pokes out under Jenny's armpit. I tickle the exposed foot. It jiggles and she giggles. I tuck it in to keep her warm. Jenny's dragging Valentino towards me. I take a step back but they keep coming. Valentino has a look of determination in his eye and a half melted chocolate bar in his hand. Jenny straps a kiddie handcuff to his wrist and attaches the other end to the pushchair. They march towards the lifts. I keep back. They don't notice that I'm not with them. I get back in the car and catch my breath.

CHAPTER 11 - DOVES

It's Christmas. It's a year since my mother died. It seems like a lot longer than that, but it's not. It's been a tough year. The worst year imaginable. I've survived, just. Dad hasn't. He's alive but he doesn't live anymore. He performs all the basic animal actions but no more than absolutely necessary. He sleeps, occasionally. Mainly with the help of drugs or alcohol. He eats, occasionally. But it's a struggle. He can't seem to muster the effort. It's painful to watch. A year ago today I lost two parents, not one.

I can't cry. I won't cry.

I check my handbag for my purse, my keys, my phone. I switch it off. I don't want to talk to anyone today. I shove my carrier bag of bits into my handbag. I pull the zip tight. It doesn't close all the way. It'll have to do; I don't have time to get another one. It's raining. My umbrella is broken and I still haven't gotten around to buying a new one. Today I don't mind. I pull my hood up over my unwashed hair and walk out into the afternoon. It's not too cold which I'm glad of.

The bus is late. I huddle under the shelter and stand next to a lady wearing a long pink raincoat. She's holding a supermarket carrier bag in her left hand. Her fingers have turned white. A man bustles in behind me. He's talking loudly on his mobile phone. He's complaining about his job. He talks in metaphors and clichés and laughs from his stomach in a booming rumble. He throws his head back when he does this. He wears the scars of last night's love-making on his shirt collar. The lady wearing the long pink raincoat rolls her eyes and sighs, shifting the carrier bag into her other hand. She nuzzles her empty hand into her pocket. The man on the phone sneezes. He doesn't cover his mouth or nose.

The bus splashes to a stop at the kerb. Two reluctant passengers stumble into the weather. The man on the phone barges past me, knocking into my arm. I let him. The lady in the long pink raincoat isn't as nice. She whacks him on the knee with her carrier bag and whatever the heavy contents may be. He swears at her but he still doesn't remove his phone from the side of his face. She ignores him and gets on the bus. He moans about the rudeness of the elderly to the voice at the other end of his connection. I can't help but chuckle. He tosses me a dirty look.

The bus is empty apart from the man on the phone, the lady in the long pink raincoat and a young couple cuddling up on the back seat. I'm jealous of them. I miss that feeling. But I can't be selfish today. It's about Mum today. I sit at the front next to the window. It's cold. I rub my hands together. It doesn't help much. I don't know if the man is still talking. My ears have tuned in to the sound of the rain working around the rumble of the world outside the bus. I shut my eyes and listen to the crash of waves as tyres speed through puddles.

I push the button on the hand rail in front of me. The bell rings and the 'bus stopping' light pings on. I stand up and stumble as the bus brakes to a stop. It's stopped raining. The three o'clock air pushes towards me and slaps me across the face as the bus doors sigh open. I step backwards and then forwards and hop fairly gracefully onto the pavement.

The church looks so small in the distance. The trees have shed their rusty finery. I manoeuvre my way through the soggy mulch of leaves adorning the base of their trunks. A man in a bright yellow sou'wester walks past me on the grass. His Wellington boots get sucked into the earth and he stumbles as he pulls himself free. He mumbles, "G'arf'noon." I assume it's intended for me as there's no-one else around. I return a smile even though I know he can't see me. I stare up at the clock tower. It's three fifteen. The sun is failing to make its way through the crowd of clouds.

I walk the path around the church. The gravel crunches underfoot. I make a conscious effort to follow the route through the baby graveyard just to remind myself that my life isn't so bad. The tiny gravestones peep out from behind bunches of flowers as if they are playing hide and seek. There are no winners.

Jessie Malone, beloved daughter, born July eleventh nineteen eighty-seven, died October eighteenth nineteen eighty-seven. A grubby looking teddy bear rests up against a small angel statue. An awkward posy droops, heavy from the rain. Andrew Arthur Nicholson, an angel has returned to heaven, born January twenty-fourth nineteen ninety-nine, died February thirteenth two thousand and six. A perfectly symmetrical Lego construction sits neatly at the base of the headstone. It looks like a rocket. Lilian was two when she died. Michael was seven. Edward, six months, and Rachael, four, were brother and sister. Are brother and sister.

I touch a moss covered stone. I try to read the name and dates but it's too worn to recognise the symbols engraved in the concrete. No-one has loved this plot for years.

I see Mum. She's as pretty as usual. The brightest one in the row. My sister Jenny does her up, fixes her foliage, washes her stone, prunes, and weeds and organises her section every week. She never lets Mum look dishevelled or worn out. Mum sparkles as she always sparkled. The two doves etched into the marble glide skywards.

I don't have flowers. I don't need them. Jenny has covered the base of Mum's headstone with poinsettias. They're still red. I don't touch them. I remember the carrier bag stuffed into my handbag. I pull it out. It explodes tinsel and baubles all over the ground. I decorate her. She wouldn't want a Christmas to go by without making a garishly gaudy effort. She looks like a drunk Christmas tree. She wouldn't have wanted it any other way.

I kneel at her feet. The ground is damp and seeps through my jeans. I speak to her inside my head. I know she's not there and I know she's not listening. That's why I stay silent. I remember her smile and her smell and her cigarette stained fingers and those annoying motion sensor Christmas characters. I laugh. I should have brought one along to keep her company, or if nothing else to terrify the other mourners whenever there was a gust of wind or a car door slamming.

The wind thrashes my hair into my eyes. It stings. My eyes water. I wipe the tears away quickly. I don't want people to think I've been crying. I look around the yard. There are no other people. I know it's cold but I don't feel it. The clock tower reminds me of the passing of time. It's just after four.

I walk home. The night has already made its appearance. The roads are quiet with school buses in hibernation. There is a giant Christmas tree in the middle of the town. It's not a real tree. Its lights are all blue. It makes me feel sad and the cold suddenly surges through my bones. The pubs are buzzing with after work business people. A door creaks open to my left and a drunk girl runs out sobbing. She's wearing a trouser suit and Doc Martens. Her cheeks are red. She can't be much more than nineteen years old. A man follows her. Their feet splash away the kebab shop lights.

My front garden gate is swinging open. I see an envelope poking out of my letterbox. The protruding end is soggy. I push it all the way through and hear it plop on the mat. The door has swollen in the rain. I use my shoulder as a battering ram and force my way into my home. Friday waits outside. It's had enough of me.

CHAPTER 12 – COLLY BIRDS

It's Christmas. It's dark outside. It's dark inside. It's dark inside me. I've not seen one person walk past my house today. They must be at home. With their families. With their friends. Must be nice.

The birds fly past. The birds fly past and they take no notice of me. I notice them but they don't return the compliment. The trees are bare. They're tall and naked. They claw at the sky with jagged talons. Witches' fingers. Nails scraping down a blackboard night sky. They make me shudder. They wave at me, those bony hands, those skeletal hands, deformed and destitute. All knuckles and empty promises.

I drink to warm myself up. To spark a light. I drink red wine. I don't get drunk anymore. I don't celebrate. What is there to celebrate? Unless people celebrate loneliness. Which I'm sure they don't. I drink to numb the pain but I don't know how much more I can drink.

There's a plastic bag stuttering in one of the trees. It moves as if it was breathing, puffing on a cigarette, blowing out birthday candles, whistling at a pretty girl as she walks by. No pretty girls walk by. No-one walks by. No-one. My reflection passes my window from the inside but it's as dark as the moon inspired shadows that paint the earth from here to sunrise.

My wine bottle is empty. Who drank it all? Was it me? I'm not drunk so it can't have been me. It must have been my guests. I look at the empty chairs around my dining table. I wonder what Oliver's doing; if he remarried, if he's spending Christmas with the children and grandchildren that I couldn't give him.

There's nothing on the television, except for a faux gold carriage clock with no battery; the time will always be seven twenty-three, and an asymmetric wooden photo frame which houses a six by four print of a smiling family recorded forever more in classic black and white. Ha, I jest. There's nothing worth watching on the television, but there never is at this time of year. Stories of hope and happiness and joy and life and togetherness. Vomit inducing drivel that I can do without.

I sleep. I don't know for how long. It's seven twenty-three all year round. I wake up to find myself curled up in the foetal position on the floor. I don't even remember lying down. I've been lying on my left arm. The pain is indescribable. My fingers tingle with flames dancing over my skin. I frantically shake them to put out the fire but that makes my hand hurt more. A fist refuses to form and my fingers lollop lifelessly by my side. I laugh. I laugh out loud. It's not funny but I laugh. I laugh so much that I fall back to the floor and lay on my back, waving my limbs like a tortoise trying to flip itself over. I laugh some more. I cry. The pain won't stop. And then it does stop. It's as though the pain was never there in the first place.

I move towards the window as if I'm going to shut the curtains. I have no intention of shutting the curtains but I rest my hands of the fabric nonetheless. I peer out through the gap and notice that the snow blanketing the path has been disturbed by footprints. They're not my footprints. I know that for a fact. And yet I still check my feet and my boots by the front door with a glance over my shoulder. They're clean. I turn back to face the window. Eyes look me square in the eyes. I jump back. The eyes jump back. They're my eyes. I still must be tired.

The air outside creaks and stretches. I do the same. I'm tired but I'm not tired. It's just boredom. Or it's the red wine. I pull the fridge door towards me. The light inside is blinding. Coloured dots dance across my retinas for a split second while my head tries to come to terms with the pounding thud that hits my skull at regular intervals. One packet of ham, unopened. One block of cheese, unwrapped. Two strawberry yoghurts that will end up going out of date. I don't like strawberries but you have to buy yogurts in packs of six and I love the peach and raspberry flavours. Half a loaf of brown bread. Three eggs. I make an omelette and I make some toast. I put the plate of food down on the dining room table and walk away.

I still haven't closed my curtains. There's no need to. No-one ever walks past. I've got no need to hide. I'm not ashamed. The snow looks blue in the first light of the morning. It's seven twenty-three. I shut my eyes. The birds tell me it's morning. They call to me to go outside. I slip my feet into my boots and wrap my father's old duffle coat around me. I say it's black. He says it's grey. We disagree over so much more than this. The door's not locked. It's never locked. I turn the handle and it clicks out of place. The door yawns open and sucks in the cold morning. I shiver and thrust my hands into the pockets of my father's old duffle coat. It's warm and soft and smells like the cigars he used to smoke at Christmas. My fingernail shudders against the sandpaper striking strip on a box of matches. My teeth chatter. I bite my tongue.

There are a few blackbirds perching like warts on the witches' fingers. I can't make out their eyes but I know they're looking at me. I clap my hands. I definitely know they're looking at me now. The ground breaks underneath my feet. I love how temporary the destruction of nature can be. This is what gives me hope.

3895867R00048

Printed in Great Britain
by Amazon.co.uk, Ltd.,
Marston Gate.